# THE PET

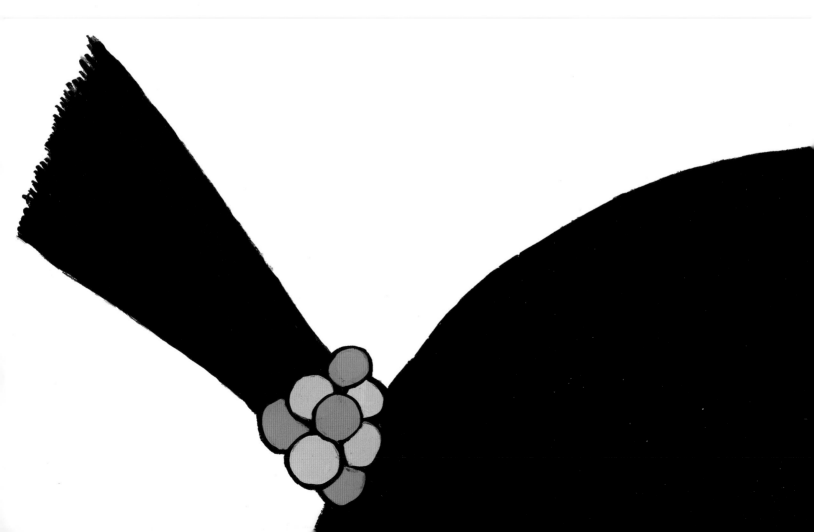

# PROJECT

## Cute and Cuddly Vicious Verses

written by Lisa Wheeler

illustrated by
Zachariah OHora

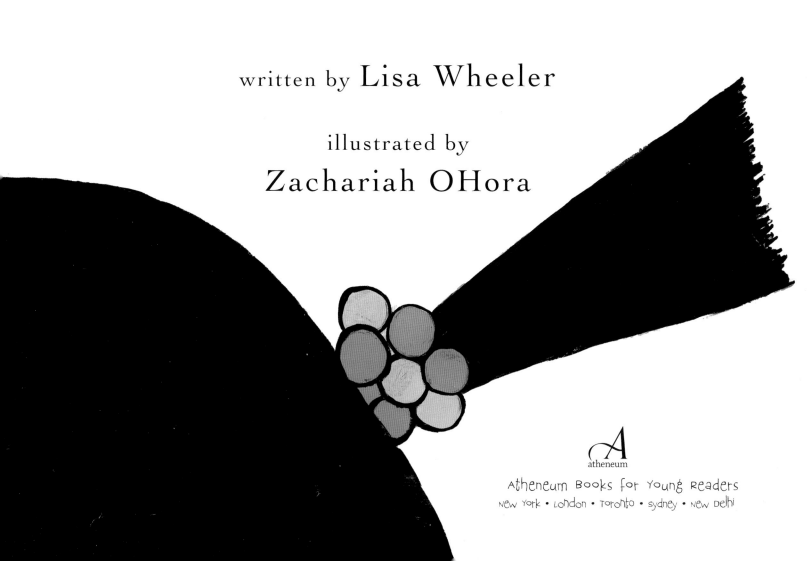

$\mathbb{A}$
atheneum

Atheneum Books for Young Readers
New York • London • Toronto • Sydney • New Delhi

For my science-minded son, Shane
— L. W.

For Kitten and the Two Bears
— Z. O.

ATHENEUM BOOKS FOR YOUNG READERS
An imprint of Simon & Schuster Children's
Publishing Division
1230 Avenue of the Americas, New York, New York 10020
Text copyright © 2013 by Lisa Wheeler
Illustrations copyright © 2013 by Zachariah OHora
ATHENEUM BOOKS FOR YOUNG READERS is a registered
trademark of Simon & Schuster, Inc.
Atheneum logo is a trademark of Simon & Schuster, Inc.
For information about special discounts for bulk purchases,
please contact Simon & Schuster Special Sales at
1-866-506-1949 or business@simonandschuster.com.
The Simon & Schuster Speakers Bureau can bring
authors to your live event. For more information or to
book an event, contact the Simon & Schuster Speakers
Bureau at 1-866-248-3049 or visit our website at
www.simonspeakers.com.
Book design by Ann Bobco
The text for this book is set in Cochin.
The illustrations for this book are rendered in acrylic paint
on bristol board.
Manufactured in China
0113 SCP
First Edition
10 9 8 7 6 5 4 3 2 1
Library of Congress Cataloging-in-Publication Data
Wheeler, Lisa.
The pet project : cute and cuddly vicious verses / Lisa
Wheeler ; illustrated by Zachariah OHora. — 1st ed.
p. cm.
Summary: The child of two scientists sets out to do
research into what sort of an animal would make the best
pet and reaches a surprising conclusion.
ISBN 978-1-4169-7595-3 (hardcover)
ISBN 978-1-4424-4234-4 (eBook)
[1. Stories in rhyme. 2. Pets—Fiction. 3. Animals—
Fiction.] I. OHora, Zachariah, ill. II. Title.
PZ8.3.W5668Pet 2013
[E]—dc23   2011029647

If you're the type who oohs and aahs
at furry faces, precious paws,
the words ahead may be alarming:

Animals aren't always charming.

I asked my parents for a pet.
My parents answered, *"Not quite yet."*

They're very science-minded folk.
*"Research, child, is not a joke."*

They told me, *"Formulate a query.
Slowly plan your bestiary."*

They said my facts should be complete.
*"Calculate what beasties eat."*

They urged me to learn all I can.
*"Devise a scientific plan."*

They added to this conversation.
*"Write down every observation."*

Then they handed me a pen.
*"When you're through, we'll talk again."*

QUERY:
what is the best pet for me?

once my query was revealed,

I prepped to study in the field.

I tucked a notebook under my arm.

Desired destination:
• farm

# COW

From the side of the road
she looked so serene,
happily chewing her cud.

Upon closer inspection
she seemed sort of mean,
nudging me into the mud.

From the side of the road
I breathed the fresh air,
the grass and the rye smelled so sweet.

Upon closer inspection
I smelled dairy air
as the cow dropped a pie at my feet.

# chicken

Hello, chickie!
You're so cute—
a puffball in a yellow suit.
Cupped in my hand you chirp and cheep.
I'll take you home, sweet little peep.
When you're grown, let's make a deal.
You'll lay an egg for every meal.
How ideal!

There's your mom! I'm gonna guess
that she has eggs inside her nest.
I'll help myself.
She shouldn't mind. . . .

*Then Mama sneaks up
from behind.*

As I search her feathered bed
that dumb cluck squawks
    and pecks my head!
Next she lunges at my legs.
Good-bye, chickie!
Keep the eggs!

# Pony

## WEEK 1

I got a pretty pony
to pet and brush and ride.
I braid his tail.
We walk the trail.
He stays right by my side.

## WEEK 2

I love my pretty pony.
He's precious and he's dear.
He stomped my toes.
He nipped my nose.
He kicked me in the ear!

## WEEK 3

### CLASSIFIED AD

Would you like a pony
to have and hold and keep?
He seldom fights.
He rarely bites. . . .

I'll sell him to you cheap.

# dove

Lovey-dovey, dovey-lovey —
cooing in the tree.

They're pigeons (only prettier)
who love to poo on me.

# sheep

You look so soft and huggable,
so sweater set and ruggable.
You sheep seem downright snuggable.
I hope you are for sale.

But as your flock gets near to us
I whiff something odiferous.
My nostrils get a snifferous.
What is that awful smell?

I know that it's regrettable.
I don't find you that pettable.
Your stink is quite upsettable.
Here comes a fainting spell!

You grin like I'm a wimp and yet
a sheep that reeks won't be my pet.
If I should feel affectionate,
I'll hug my rug and sweater set.

The farm was interesting, and yet
I still have failed to find a pet.
Sure of what I have to do,
I'll take my research to the

- ~~farm~~
- zoo

# monKey

He looks so like a little man
    with smiling teeth and grasping hand.
He chatters to his monkey friends,
    but that is where the likeness ends.
His fur is full of bugs and lice.
    He flings his poo — His aim's precise.
His scream sounds like a banshee's wail.
    He swings from his prehensile tail.
And worst of all he smells so funky.
    If he's a man, then I'm a monkey!

## tiger

Never take a tiger home,
no matter how he pleads with you,
'cause if you take a tiger home,
we'll soon see how he feeds with you.

# penguin

You're the emperor of cute,
with waddly walk and pouty beak.
Strutting in your birthday suit,
make-believing you're unique.

Blending in with all the others,
have you joined a club of clones?
Stamped and shaped by cookie cutters,
do you ever walk alone?

It's a penguin hall of mirrors,
fading in and out of sight.
No one is as he appears
in a sea of black and white.

Every time I blink, I lose you
in this world of ice and snow.
If you hide, how can I choose you?
Penguin?
Penguin?
Where'd you go?

# hippopotamus

Chances of getting a hippo:
zippo.

# polar
# bear

Cuddly wuddly polar bear,
whatcha doin' over there?
Whatcha holdin' in your paws?
Whatcha puttin' in your jaws?
Whatcha munchin'?
Whatcha crunchin'?

*Yuck!*

I'm done lunchin'.

completely finished with the zoo,
I think I need a fresher view.
I do not have that far to roam.
I'll try the woods behind my home.

# skunk

With lovely face and fluffy tail,
the she-skunk seeks to meet a male.
No matter what the he-skunk thinks,
I think the she-skunk truly stinks.

# squirrels

All the squirrels up in our tree
are fond of making fun of me.
For when they see me cutting grass
or raking leaves, they laugh and laugh.

I think it might be supercool
if every squirrel came with a tool.
Perhaps some clippers or a mower,
garden sheers, electric blower.

When they came down from our tree
I would make them work for me.
As I watched them mowing grass,
I'd climb our tree, then laugh and laugh.

# bunnies

Long, fuzzy ears and baskets of eggs,
light fluffy tails and strong, bouncy legs.
*Hippety-skippity*
*Hoppity-hop.*

STOP!

Garden warriors
plan the attack.
Ready for action.
Don't turn your back!

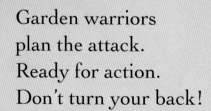

Steadfast fur soldiers,
armed to the teeth,
nibble your lettuce
above and beneath,
conquering cabbages
row upon row,

destroying your carrots
before they can grow.
Ravaging radishes,
pillaging peas,
taking your turnips—
They do as they please!

Their cute reputations
are rabbity lies.
They're voracious Vikings
in bunny disguise!

Though they all have lovely features,
I'm not charmed by woodland creatures.
Before true testing can begin,
I have to bring some beasties in.

## TEST SUBJECT #1:

# goldfish

It seemed so sweet and innocent—
worth the silver coins I spent.

I filled the bowl and took a seat.
Then I watched it overeat.

It ate and ate until it bloated.
Up and up and up it floated.

Now it ceases to exist.
I scratched the goldfish off my list.

## TEST SUBJECT #2:
# ant farm

He's like a teeny alien
dressed up in body armor.
Imposter with antennae,
who pretends to be a farmer.

Has he ever plowed a field?
Has he milked a cow?
I watched his kind for days
    and days.
Not one of them knew how.

Pretend to be so innocent,
those crawling little dots.
All the while they dream
    their schemes
and make their fiendish
    plots.

They bide their time behind
    the glass
and plan for bigger things,
when aliens disguised as ants
will rule the world as kings!

## TEST SUBJECT #3:
# small dog

A little dog might work for me —
a trendy, hip accessory.
I'd carry her each place I roam.
My backpack would become her home.
And all the kids would think it cool
that I could wear my dog to school.

But what would it be like down there,
stuffed in a backpack, short on air?
No exercise, deprived of smells,
the victim of my show-'n'-tells.
No dog should be so tightly penned.
Who would do that to a friend?

# TEST SUBJECT #4:
# kitten

Pitter-patter pampered paws,
   *ripping razor cutting claws,*
pretty, pinky, pouty mouth.
   *Simply shredded leather couch,*
whisper whisker kitty kiss.
   *Horrific high-pitched spitting hiss,*
precious, pretty cuddle cat,
   *precocious, spoiled, crabby brat.*

When a kitten is your pet,
   you never know what you will get.
One minute it's as sweet as pie,
   the next, it's swatting at your eye.
Its personality is split.
   I think I best get rid of it.

somehow my parents figured out
what all the cages were about.
In order to escape their fuss
I'm taking notes at Pets "R" us.

# turtle

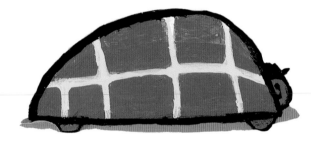

The turtle seems a boring pet.
He sits there in his bowl.
He doesn't beg. He doesn't run.
He doesn't even roll.

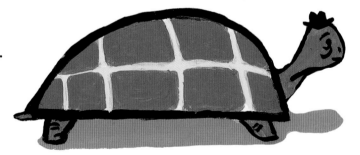

The turtle has a boring shell.
No feathers, fur, or fuzz.
The problem with a turtle is
He *doesn't* more than *does*.

# gerbils

They once were known as "desert rats."
They like to gnaw and chew.

The book says they are sociable—
It's best if I get two.

But if I get a he and she,
therein the troubles lie.

Instead of two, I'd soon have ten.
These creatures multiply!

I'd have to care for more and more,
litter after litter.

I think I'll quit while I'm ahead
and choose another critter.

# guinea pig

I'm studying this guinea pig.
He makes a funny squeak.

He's not a pig. He's not a mouse.
(Some hybrid mutant freak?)

His ears are small. He has no tail.
His fur is short and thick.

Oh yuck! He tinkled in my hand.
I think I might be sick.

ICK!

Hey, you intrepid reporter!

I'm talking to you!!

# parrot

The parrot at the pet store
is the color of a cherry,
with blue and yellow wingtips
and a large vocabulary.

He's memorized some sonnets
and some long Shakespearian verses.
But when I try to talk to him
that *fowl* mouth only curses!

# mice

## oBSERVATiON

The pet store has a lot of mice.
I wait to see who buys them.
Mice, it seems, are plentiful.
It's nature that supplies them.

## QUERY

If mice are truly bountiful,
then why do people get them?
It seems it would be cheaper
just to buy live traps and set them.

Note: Ask shop guy why they carry so many mice.

# snake

The big, fat snake seems rather nice.
I watch the shop guy feed him . . .

## GULP!

Never mind.

The pet store had an awful smell.
It was a noisy place, as well.
Who knew the work this quest
involved?
My query is still unresolved.

# pet rock

My father said he had a rock —
a rock that was his pet.
This goes to show that long ago
Dad wasn't too smart yet.
He must be more intelligent
now that he is older.
But just for fun, last Father's Day,
I gave him a pet boulder.

# disappointments

I met a golden retriever.
He never brought me gold.
The starfish didn't twinkle.
The *New*foundland was *old*.

Can't rope and ride the bullfrog.
The hedgehog isn't hoggish.
No dragon in a dragonfly.
The prairie dog's not doggish.

Carpenter ants aren't builders.
Pinschers never pinch.
Boxers have no boxing gloves.
An inchworm's not an inch.

I find this all confusing,
but research doesn't lie.

*No chocolate in a chocolate Lab?*

I think I'm gonna cry!

# conclusions

My research gave me food for
   thought.
I know what kind of kid I'm not.
I'm not the kind for mucking stalls
or brushing fur
or throwing balls
or cleaning bowls
or clipping nails
or watching out
for wagging tails.

I am the sort who soon forgets,
and that's not good when you've got
   pets.

But . . .

My research found
that all around
tiny animals abound.

They need no care.
They need no fuss.
They're not aware
that there is *us*.

These beasties who are hard to find
are *everywhere* . . . and they're all
mine!

I go to Mom and Dad with hope:

*"May I have a microscope?"*